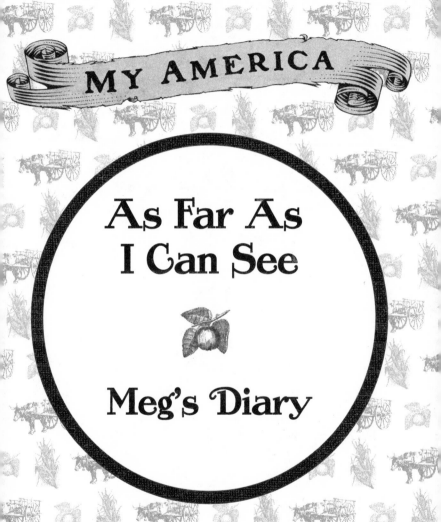

MY AMERICA

As Far As I Can See

Meg's Diary

by Kate McMullan

Scholastic Inc. New York

St. Louis, Missouri
1856

May 15, 1856

I am Margaret Cora Wells, also known as Meg. I have never before kept a diary. Mother gave me this one for my ninth birthday. I only wish it had a lock. That way I could keep out my nosy seven-year-old brother, also known as Preston.

May 16, 1856

Nothing exciting happened today. But soon I hope to write about these adventures:

1. Boating with my best friend, Julia

2. Acting in my school's spring play, *The Tempest*
3. Going to church wearing one of the fashionable, new hoopskirts, also known as a "cage"

May 17, 1856

This afternoon, Mother told me to dress for a birthday surprise! I put on my white stockings, lace pantalettes, and four petticoats. Nellie slipped my lilac silk dress over my head. She fastened all twenty-four buttons down my back with her buttonhook.

I came downstairs. Father had hitched Brownie and Bess to the open carriage. I climbed in beside Mother and Preston. Grace had to stay home. She is only four and, Mother says, too young for excitement. Nellie held her, and she waved as we drove off.

The horses' hooves clip-clopped on the cobblestones as we rode to the riverfront. So much was going on! Men moved boxes and trunks. They blew horns to say, "Get out of my way!" Pres kept standing up to see. Twice he nearly fell out of the carriage.

A whole city of steamboats was docked at the Mississippi River landing. Their smoke-stacks reached up to the clouds. Father calls them *"floating palaces."* How I wish to ride on one some day.

Father stopped the carriage in front of the new Barnum's City Hotel. It has just been built, right in the spot where so many buildings burned down in the Fire of 1849. The hotel is very tall — six stories high!

We went into Barnum's ice-cream parlor. It had pink-and-white striped paper on the walls. I ordered peppermint ice cream. It was delicious and it matched the wallpaper exactly. I wish it had matched my dress for, I am sorry to say, I dripped a little on my front.

Pres chose chocolate. He even had seconds. Mother said his chin was a disgrace.

I am now seated on a blue velvet chair. Mother and I are in the hotel lobby. We are waiting for Father and Pres to bring the carriage. Next to my chair is a palm tree in a pot. When I am older, I hope to spend a night in this hotel.

I am fond of luxury. Too fond, Mother says. But even Mother is enjoying herself this afternoon. How good to see her smile for a change.

Later

I saw something terrible!

I will never forget it as long as I live.

When we left the hotel, our carriage became stuck in a jam of carriages and carts. We did not move for a long time.

We saw that a crowd had gathered at the Courthouse. Father got out and walked ahead to see what was happening.

Pres said his stomach hurt. Mother said it was from too much ice cream. She said if he was going to be sick, he must jump out of the carriage.

At that, Pres jumped out! He was not sick, but he took off running through the crowd.

Mother called after him to come back.

But Pres kept going.

So I jumped out of the carriage and ran after him. I got hot from running. My petticoats were peppered with soot. How I wished Pres had stayed home with Grace!

I ran after my brother. But I could not catch him. He ducked under people's elbows. He wove through the crowd. Then he stopped short, and I nearly bumped into him.

I grabbed his hand but he yanked it away.

Pres stood in front of the Courthouse. He stared up at a Negro family on the steps — a father, a mother, and a young daughter.

A man's loud voice startled me. It called out, "Tom! Show how you walk."

The Negro man walked. He moved stiffly. Then I saw why. He had iron chains on his ankles.

I did not understand what I was seeing, but I knew it was awful. The little girl looked so frightened. I tried to pull Pres away, but he would not be pulled.

"Bidders!" the man called. I saw that he held a whip. "Come feel Tom's muscles. He can lift heavy boxes. He has years of hard work left in him yet. Buy him alone or with his wife, a fine house slave."

Now I knew what was happening. Tom was a slave. He was being sold!

A hand clamped onto my shoulder. It spun me around, and I saw no more. I looked up at my father's red, angry face. He was glaring at the scene on the steps.

He kept one hand on my shoulder and the other on Preston's. He hurried us back to the carriage.

I cried all the way home.

Bedtime

Mother came to tuck me in tonight. My voice shook as I asked how one person could be sold to another. Mother said what I have heard her say before: that slavery is a terrible evil. She said many people called abolitionists are working hard to end slavery, to make it against the law. They help slaves run away from states where slavery is allowed. They help them ride on the Underground Railroad. "It is not really a train," Mother said, "but a series of secret hiding places called 'stations.'" People called "conductors" take the slaves from station to station, all the way to freedom.

Oh, how I hope Tom and his family will find a way to ride on the Underground Railroad!

May 22, 1856

Grace cried much of last night. Mother says she has a little fever.

May 23, 1856

Grace cannot keep her food down. She cries from stomach pains. Mother tries not to show it, but I can tell that she is very worried.

Later

I came home from school and found Mother busy tending to Grace. So I have come into the parlor to look at the photographs on the piano. One is in a case lined with blue velvet. It shows my aunt Margaret. She is Mother's younger sister. I am named for her but I look nothing like her. Aunt Margaret has a round face and light hair. My face is narrow and my hair is red, like Father's.

Aunt Margaret, Uncle Aubert, and their boys moved to Kansas Territory two years ago. It is not even part of the United States! Mother says Uncle Aubert moved because he wanted to own land, and her poor dear baby sister had to follow him to Kansas, windy Kansas. Also known as "the end of the earth."

Another picture is in a case with black velvet. It shows small twin boys. They are holding hands. They are my brothers, Lee and Larry. They caught cholera in the terrible epidemic of 1849. I once heard Father say that the twins fell sick in the morning and by nightfall, they were dead. Thousands of people in St. Louis died of cholera that summer. I was only two years old. I cannot remember Lee and Larry. But Mother never forgets them, not ever.

Preston just ran into the parlor. He is pulling his kite, shouting for it to "Fly, fly, fly!"

My friend Julia says that just watching Preston can wear a person out.

May 24, 1856

Something awful has happened. Mother has come down sick. No one says the word "cholera." But I can hear it in the silence.

I am very frightened.

May 25, 1856

I heard Father's footsteps on the floor above my bedroom last night. Back and forth, back and forth, all night long.

Today is Sunday, but we did not go to church. Father let his egg and toast grow cold at breakfast while he stared out the window. The boughs of Mother's apple trees are heavy with blooms. But I could tell that Father did not see the flowers.

I am not allowed in the sickrooms so I have come out to the garden. Bees buzz above me as I write. The apple blossoms smell sweet and sad at the same time.

Later

I overheard Father tell Nellie that Mother is out of her head with worry over Preston and me. He said that if we came down with cholera, it would kill Mother. She fears that another epidemic will strike St. Louis this summer. She has made Father promise to send us away until fall. Away! But where?

Later

I write by candlelight. If Nellie catches me, she will scold. She will tell me how a breeze can blow a window curtain into a candle flame. It can start a terrible fire. But I am too hot to sleep. The netting over my bed seems to keep out air as well as mosquitoes.

I pray that Mother will not send us away. I want to stay here to write in my diary: *Mother and Grace are well again.*

May 26, 1856

Mother has not changed her mind. Tonight at supper Father had news for Preston and me. We are going to Kansas to stay with Aunt Margaret for the summer.

Pres whooped. He said he could not wait to fly his kite in windy Kansas.

Preston is an ignorant little boy. I wish he were sick instead of Mother and Grace.

Later

I do not wish that Preston were sick. I could never wish that.

May 27, 1856

Father has worked fast. His friend Dr. Baer is moving to Kansas. To a place called Neosho.

Father says Dr. Baer is a "vegetarian." He eats vegetables, but no meat. Neosho, Kansas, is a place especially for vegetarians. It has a fine climate, so the vegetarians can grow all their own food. Dr. Baer showed Father a pamphlet. It told of the wonders of Neosho.

Dr. Baer has a ticket to ride on a steamboat, *The Kansas Hopeful*. Father has bought tickets for Preston and me, too. We will travel to Kansas City with Dr. Baer to watch over us. Then Dr. Baer will drive us to Aunt Margaret's house as it is on the way to Neosho.

We leave tomorrow morning!

Julia cannot even come to tell me good-bye. Her mother will not let her come into a house where there is sickness.

Father and Pres have gone to Shapleigh, Day & Co., the hardware store downtown. They are buying seeds, skillets, nails, cloth, linens, and blankets for us to take to Aunt

Margaret and Uncle Aubert. Mother wants us to take her baby apple tree seedlings, too.

Nellie and I have been packing all day. I will take:

1 lilac silk dress	6 pr. stockings
1 cream silk dress	2 pr. shoes
1 rose silk dress	1 pr. boots
1 blue linen dress	1 wool coat
3 camisoles	1 pr. gloves
2 pr. pantalettes	1 night dress
6 petticoats	1 diary

Bedtime

Dr. Baer came over tonight. He has a thick moustache and bushy whiskers. He looks just like a great, hairy-faced bear! His German accent makes him hard to understand. I do not want to be looked after by a bear.

I said good night to Father. I curtsied to Dr. Baer. As I started up to bed, I heard Dr. Baer say that Kansas is a dangerous place right now. I stopped on the stairs to listen. I heard Father say, "Margaret is the only family we have outside St. Louis. Besides, nothing is as dangerous as cholera."

I wanted to hear more. But Nellie took my hand. She led me upstairs. She said I might go to the door of Mother's sickroom to say good-bye.

I stood at the door. Mother was in bed. I tried not to cry, but tears ran down my cheeks.

"Do not let Preston out of your sight," Mother said.

I promised I would not.

"Be a good help to Aunt Margaret," Mother said.

I promised I would.

Then Mother said something surprising:

"Keep your diary, Meg. I want to read about your Kansas adventures when you come home."

. . . *when you come home*. . . .

How good those words sounded to me! I pictured it in my mind. Mother and I, sitting in the parlor, laughing over my time in windy Kansas.

I promised to write everything down in my diary.

Nellie led me from the door. She put her arms around me. She held me while I cried. I said I could not stand to be so far from home. Nellie said yes, I could. After all, she had come all the way from Ireland, across the sea. And she is doing fine. I cried even harder then, thinking of Nellie here, and her family so far away.

I am on a steamboat — a floating palace! I am on the upper deck, looking out over all of St. Louis. Not long ago, I wished to be here. Now my wish has come true. But I never wished it to happen this way!

Nellie shook me awake before dawn. I dressed quickly. She held a lantern as she rushed Pres and me down the walk. Father had the carriage waiting. Nellie put a basket of journey food into my lap. She hugged me hard. Then off we raced to the levee.

Even at dawn, the levee was noisy and crowded. Father hurried Pres and me aboard *The Kansas Hopeful*. He made sure that our trunks and the baby apple trees were stored below deck with the rest of the baggage and with the horses, cows, and chickens that are traveling to Kansas. Then Father found Dr.

Baer and put us in his care. A gong rang. All who were not going had to get off the boat. I hugged Father good-bye. It was so very hard to let him go! I said Mother's words inside my head: *When you come home . . . When you come home . . .*

Pres and I stood at the rail. We watched Father walk down the plank. I held back my tears, as I did not want to upset Pres. But he waved and shouted happily to Father. I should know better than to worry about upsetting Preston.

The boat engines roared. Great clouds of smoke poured from the smoke-stacks. The big paddle wheel of *The Kansas Hopeful* began to turn, and we pulled out into the Mississippi River. The boat rose and fell in the water. It gave me the strangest feeling in my stomach.

I waved until I could no longer see Father. I watched the steeples and chimneys until they disappeared. Then all I could see was a cloud of smoke hanging over what I knew to be St. Louis. Good-bye Father! Get well, Mother and Grace!

Later

We had hardly left the dock when Preston dragged Dr. Baer and me off to explore the boat. We climbed a wide staircase to the grand saloon. It has red carpeting and red velvet curtains. It is every bit as fancy as Barnum's City Hotel.

We saw several tables where men and women sat, playing cards. One player stood out from the others. He was tall. His yellow hair hung down past his shoulders. He wore a black cloak. And his eyes! One was blue and the other, brown! Pres whispered to me that the man was surely an outlaw and that he was hiding a pistol under his cloak.

At the far end of the saloon, waiters began bringing out platters with roasts and sliced meats and potatoes. There were bowls of stew and many kinds of fish. They set them over flames to keep them hot. They also set out coffee, tea, cakes, pastries, nuts, and candies. Pres was almost drooling as he watched.

We were startled by a clanging gong. People ran into the saloon. It was a stampede! Men pushed and shoved to get a seat. They lunged across the tables to grab the dishes.

At last Dr. Baer, Pres, and I found seats, but by then the food was all gone! The waiters had started to clear the tables.

We were lucky we had our basket of journey food. (Oh, bless you, Nellie, for tucking in the photographs of Mother, Father, and Grace. And the one of yourself, too, dear Nellie!)

After we ate, we found an empty bench out on the deck. We are sitting there now, watching the passengers.

Many women pass by with their children. Dr. Baer says they are going to meet their husbands, who have staked "claims" of land in the west.

A woman in a green dress with a hoopskirt strolled by. A young Negro girl tried to hold a matching green parasol over her head. But the girl was not very tall. She could not hold the parasol steady. The woman shouted, "Keep the sun off my face! Or I shall send you below deck to spend the rest of the trip with the cows!"

Dr. Baer shook his head. He said this poor girl was a slave, and slavery was a stain on the heart of humanity. He said it was a terrible shame that Missouri did not pass laws against it.

Pres said he would rather ride with the cows any day than with that horrid woman.

The yellow-haired gambler went by. He carried a big, heavy case. He looked over at us with his different colored eyes. It gave me the shivers.

A straight-backed woman with white hair stopped to chat with us. She is Miss Peach. She introduced us to her sixteen-year-old niece, Hannah. Hannah Peach has blonde hair and rosy cheeks. The two women have traveled all the way from New York. And just think — they are vegetarians going to Neosho! Dr. Baer and Miss Peach became instant friends.

Dr. Baer said, "There is nothing as fine as fresh vegetables."

Miss Peach said, "Amen to that!"

Dr. Baer said, "And breathing good, clean air."

Miss Peach said, "Amen to that!"

I said to myself, *I will take the smoky, dirty air of St. Louis any day.*

And I answered myself, *Amen!*

May 29, 1856

Dr. Baer and Pres slept in a Gentlemen's Cabin last night. I slept in a Ladies' Cabin. That is the rule on *The Kansas Hopeful*, so I had to let Pres out of my sight. There were ten cots in our Ladies' Cabin. I chose one next to Hannah Peach.

This morning Hannah and I dressed quickly. We ran out of the stuffy cabin to the deck. Our boat was passing bluffs with apple trees in bloom. I breathed in the scent of blossoms. I closed my eyes and said a silent prayer: *Please, Lord, help Mother and Grace get well!*

Pres and Dr. Baer found me standing at the rail. When the gong rang, we pushed, shoved, and grabbed our breakfast. How quickly we have learned riverboat manners!

We went out on the deck then. Our ship was starting its turn from the Mississippi west onto the Missouri River. A man next to me at the rail said that this is a tricky river for a steamboat. One minute it is deep, and the next, it's no more than a ripple over the sand.

The yellow-haired gambler passed by again. He carried his big case. Preston caught my eye. He whispered, "Pistols!"

A group of passengers strolled the deck, singing "Call to Kansas!" When the song ended, they talked of moving to Kansas Territory to make new homes and of voting to make Kansas a state where slavery is not allowed. How good to hear them talk this way! Now the last two lines of their song keep ringing inside my head:

> We'll sing, upon the Kansas plains,
> A song of liberty.

Later

Pres loves to watch the boat hands drop a knotted rope into the river. Dr. Baer says they do this to measure how deep the water is. The hands call out the measurement: "Three feet! Three and a half! Four feet! No bottom!"

Later

Our floating palace is tied to trees on the bank for the night. Pres and I are sitting in the saloon in front of the fire. Outside, a storm rages. Thunder roars. Lightning flashes. Rain falls in buckets. I tell Pres not to be afraid. Of course, he is not.

May 30, 1856

This morning our boat struck a sandbar. What a shock to stop so suddenly! The engines groaned, trying to pull us off the sand. It sounded as if they might explode. Then there was a second jolt. We were free of the sandbar! Everyone on *The Kansas Hopeful* cheered.

Later

This afternoon we stopped in Booneville to pick up passengers. An old woman selling apples came aboard. I bought three of them. The woman's face was brown and wrinkled.

She had no teeth. She said she was Miss Annie Boone, kin to the famous woodsman, Daniel Boone.

Suddenly, the boat began moving again. Miss Boone set up a terrible fuss. She ran to the ship's clerk and said the warning gong never rang. The clerk said yes, it did. He said Miss Boone's ears must be full of Missouri River mud. The two went back and forth like this for some time. Pres enjoyed the fight tremendously.

At last the captain steered the boat to shore. A boat hand shoved a plank out onto a bluff.

Just then the yellow-haired gambler walked over to Miss Boone. He offered his arm. He said he would walk her across the plank to the shore.

But Miss Boone shouted at him to go away! She turned and ran over the plank to the bluff.

The yellow-haired gambler stood at the rail, grinning. He waved and called farewell. But Miss Boone only shook her fist at him.

Pres says he would trade his kite to know what the gambler did to make Miss Boone so mad.

June 1, 1856

Dr. Baer, Preston, Miss Peach, Hannah, and I sat down to dinner this noon. I filled my bowl with beef stew. Suddenly everything on the table slid right into our laps! My chair toppled over. I somehow landed on my feet. Everyone was running in all directions. I grabbed Pres's hand. I could not see Dr. Baer. I had no idea what was happening.

The boat was tilted sideways. The floor was a slippery hill. Pres and I made our way up it to the high side of the boat. A steward called out that we had hit a sandbar. The engine fires were out. And the boiler was filled with sand.

Suddenly the boat rocked wildly. We were thrown to the floor. But now the floor was level again. We were free of the sandbar. I waited for the cheering. But no one cheered. Then I saw why. We were adrift! The current was swift. We were moving down the river very fast.

A steward shouted to us to get to the bow.

"If the boat smashes up," he called, "that's the best place for jumping off!"

I clutched Preston's hand and we ran. Everyone was running for the front of the boat. I worried that so many people might make the boat tip over on its nose. We reached the bow and hung onto the rail. We watched the boat hands ready the anchor.

The yellow-haired gambler stood beside us. He said if the anchor caught the shore and held, all would be well. But if it did not, the boat might spin out of control and smash into an underwater tree.

I held my breath.

The boat hands threw out the anchor. It missed the shore. It sank in the swirling water.

Quickly, the hands pulled the anchor in. They threw it out again. It sank once more.

I felt the boat turning sideways in the current.

The captain barked out commands.

My heart raced as the boat hands gathered in the rope. They threw the anchor out again. This time it caught. The boat jerked to a stop. Pres and I threw our arms around the yellow-haired gambler and cheered. Then I remembered who he was and quickly pulled Pres away.

The hands pulled on the anchor rope and brought the boat to shore. All passengers had to get off while the hands shoveled sand out of the boiler. It was odd to walk upon dry land after so many days swaying on the river.

Pres ran over and got into the footraces that some young men had organized. Hannah and I went down to the river. We splashed water on our skirts to wash out the beef stew. I fear my lilac silk will never be the same.

We strolled on the bluff then. Dr. Baer walked beside Miss Peach. He hummed "Call to Kansas!" as he walked. I have become fond of Dr. Baer.

The yellow-haired gambler stood on the shore beside his many heavy cases. I heard Dr. Baer saying something about "smuggling rifles" and "Border Ruffians." Oh, to think that Pres and I threw our arms around a rifle smuggler!

Soon the boat hands called, "All aboard!" We walked up the plank and continued on our way.

June 2, 1856

I can see Kansas City in the distance!

Pres and I have our cases packed. Dr. Baer said when the boat docks, he will hurry off to buy supplies, as he has heard that they sell out fast. Pres and I are to stay on board until the pushing and shoving are over. Then we are to walk down the plank and wait for Dr. Baer beside the boat.

Dr. Baer says we will stay in a hotel tonight. After six days on *The Kansas Hopeful,* I am ready for a bath! I long for fresh towels. And clean sheets.

Later

Pres and I are sitting on our trunks on the dock. Beside me is the tub with the baby apple trees. They are a bit wilted from being below.

Kansas City looks nothing like a city. The street is hardly more than a dirt path! It is lined with overloaded wagons heading west, out of town. Pres counted eighteen mules pulling one wagon.

A herd of cattle just thundered by! I must go grab onto Preston so he won't dash off and be trampled by a cow.

Later

The yellow-haired gambler loaded his wagon with all sorts of cases. Pres says the big cases must hold rifles. And the small ones, pistols. Then his mule team pulled his wagon away.

Miss Peach and Hannah hugged us good-bye. They have hired a Mexican driver to take them to Neosho. Hannah asked us to come visit them. Miss Peach said, "Amen to that!" Then they drove off.

Everyone has gone now — everyone but Pres and me. We are still sitting on our trunks.

Evening

Dr. Baer came at last. He said it was not easy to buy supplies in a frontier town.

We began looking for a hotel. But they all had signs that said: NO VACANCY. Finally we found a place at Grigg's Hotel. It was shabby and very crowded. But Dr. Baer said it was the best we could do. We sat down to a supper of boiled cabbage. It smelled awful. But there was nothing else, so we ate it. Dr. Baer said, "Hunger is the best sauce."

Night

We do not even have a room in this awful hotel. Only three cots in the hallway. As we came upstairs, a woman shouted, "Don't put your shoes and stockings on the floor, or the rats will carry them off!"

My feet are drawn up on my cot. Downstairs, fiddlers are playing. People are stomping and dancing and shouting, "Yahoo!"

I said to Pres, "I cannot wait to leave this hotel."

Pres said, "Amen to that!"

June 3, 1856

I did not sleep a wink. I heard little claws scratching all night long. But we waited until sunup to leave, for we did not want to step on a rat in the dark. Good riddance to Grigg's Hotel!

Morning

I am sitting in a small space in the back of an open wagon, writing as we go. Preston is sitting next to Dr. Baer on the driver's seat. The wagon is a big wooden box on wheels. It is packed with supplies and furniture that Dr. Baer had sent ahead. Our trunks are squeezed in, too. And so is the tub with Mother's baby apple trees.

Dr. Baer bought us hats to keep off the sun. Pres's hat is a small man's hat. He loves it. Mine is a sunbonnet. The brim is nearly as long as my arm! What if someone should see me in such an unfashionable bonnet? I shall never wear it.

Our wagon is pulled by two oxen, also known as Ruby and Blanco. Ruby is red. Blanco is nearly white. They sway as they walk. So does my writing.

It is forty miles to Aunt Margaret's house. Dr. Baer says he hopes to make the trip in four days.

Later

Tall prairie grass grows as far as I can see. I feel as if we are traveling over a beautiful green tablecloth. The wind blows through the grass with a lonesome whistling sound. I never knew the sky could be so big!

Later

I never knew the sun could be so hot.

Afternoon

I have put on the bonnet. The shade feels heavenly. And no one will see me in it anyway. So far we have passed only one dead, swollen cow by the side of the trail. Poor creature!

Later

Dr. Baer says we are traveling through Delaware Indian territory. Pres is keen to see a Delaware. But Dr. Baer says they are probably hunting farther west this time of year.

Later

We have stopped by a stream in the shade of some oaks. Dr. Baer tied ropes to Ruby and Blanco. The other end of each rope is attached to a spike called a picket. Dr. Baer hammered the pickets into the ground. Now Ruby and Blanco can nibble grass in a wide circle.

Dr. Baer spread a cloth on the grass. He set out jam and biscuits. I picked a bunch of blue flowers. Dr. Baer put them in water in his tin cup and set the cup on our cloth. This is what he calls a pic-nic.

Pres is chasing little jumping bugs. Dr. Baer says they are "grasshoppers."

I still love smoky St. Louis. But, my, this air smells sweet.

Bedtime

We found out something about Dr. Baer tonight. Something so sad!

We were sitting around the campfire. Preston suddenly bounced into Dr. Baer's lap.

He hugged him. Then he asked why he had no children.

I started to scold Pres. But Dr. Baer said he did not mind answering. He told us that he once had a wife and three daughters. They all died in the same cholera epidemic that killed Lee and Larry. Tears came into his eyes as he spoke.

Tears came into my eyes, too. I felt bad for Dr. Baer. And worried for Mother and Grace.

Dr. Baer said his house was once full of girls and laughter — and the rustle of petticoats. Now the house is still. Dr. Baer said he is moving to Kansas because he no longer wants to wake up in an empty house.

Pres hugged Dr. Baer again. I went over and hugged him, too. We thanked "our Bear" for watching over us on our journey.

Wolves are howling now. Dr. Baer says they are far away. I will try to believe him.

June 4, 1856

Pres and I helped Dr. Baer unload the wagon last night. We covered the supplies with an oilskin cloth. Then we climbed into the wagon box. We rolled up in Indian blankets and fell asleep under the stars.

Sometime in the night it started to rain. I scooted down in my blanket like a turtle in its shell. This morning I discovered that Pres had crawled under the wagon to stay dry. When he crawled out this morning, he was covered with mud. He said he liked mud. It was all I could do to get him to change into a clean shirt and trousers.

The trail was so muddy from the rain that our wagon wheels got stuck. Ruby and Blanco could not pull us out. So Pres and I got behind the wagon. We pushed with all our might. Dr. Baer pulled from the front with the oxen. At last the wheels began to turn. They splattered us with mud. But we cheered anyway, just as when *The Kansas Hopeful* came off the sandbar.

Preston's clean, dry clothes are now wet and muddy. My blue linen dress is mud-brown. But we shall stay dressed as we are, for we will only get muddier this day.

Mother would say we are all a disgrace.

Later

Two men on horseback came up behind us on the trail. They had rifles slung over their saddles. They stopped to talk with us. They said they were from Georgia. They asked where we came from. Dr. Baer was not at all friendly. He said only that we were from Missouri. This answer seemed to satisfy them. They went their way.

When they were gone, Dr. Baer frowned. He said the men were Border Ruffians. They and others like them are coming to Kansas to vote. They will vote for Kansas to become a state that allows slavery. Then they will go home again.

I asked why men from Georgia cared so much about Kansas. Dr. Baer said they do not care about Kansas. But they care about slavery. They want as many states as possible to allow slavery. That way they think the United States will never pass laws against it.

I think Border Ruffians are what Dr. Baer meant when he said Kansas could be dangerous.

Later

It was too windy to start a fire tonight. So we had soda biscuits for supper. They were as hard as rocks.

June 5, 1856

The mosquitoes are fierce. Pres and I are covered with bites.

We passed a pair of covered wagons on the side of the trail today. A man said they were stopping just long enough for a baby to be born!

This evening Pres and I gathered dried prairie grass. Dr. Baer used it to start a campfire. He fed it with wood he gathered when we had our pic-nic under the oaks. He set up two forked sticks on either side of the fire. He ran a long branch through the handle of an iron kettle. Then he laid the branch on the forks of the sticks. In this way he hung the kettle over the fire.

Dr. Baer poured water into the kettle. I helped him cut up carrots and potatoes. Pres plopped them into the water. Then Dr. Baer added dried herbs: parsley, thyme, and rosemary. He says that herbs are the secret to vegetarian cooking. Before long, a wonderful smell rose from the kettle. But when it was time to serve the soup, I came too close to the fire. The wind blew ash onto the hem of my rose-colored silk. It is burned with many tiny holes. In spite of this, the dinner was delicious.

My lilac silk dress is stained with soup. My blue linen is covered in mud. Now my rose-colored silk is burnt. Soon I shall have nothing to wear!

June 6, 1856

We reached the Kaw River this morning. Dr. Baer drove the wagon onto a ferry boat and it carried us across the river. We saw buildings in the distance. The ferry driver said that this is Lawrence. He said there had been fighting in the town, and the Border Ruffians burned down the hotel!

Later

Dr. Baer says we are almost there. I am all nerves now. I have on my cream silk. My last clean dress! I have brushed my hair and braided it. I want to look my best when I see Aunt Margaret.

Bedtime

We are in Aunt Margaret and Uncle Aubert's cabin. Too tired to write more.

June 7, 1856

Father's letter never arrived!
We drove up to a log cabin yesterday at

sunset. Aunt Margaret and Uncle Aubert came out to see who their visitors were. They had no idea we were coming! Tears sprang to Aunt Margaret's eyes when she saw Pres and me. She and Uncle Aubert were sad to learn the reason for our coming. But they are glad to have us. Aunt Margaret says she is happy to have another female with her, way out here on the prairie.

Aunt Margaret looks like Mother. But her hands! They are as red and chapped as Nellie's.

Dr. Baer put Ruby and Blanco on picket ropes to feed. He and Uncle Aubert unloaded our things from the wagon.

We went into the log cabin. The walls are covered with newspapers! Cousin George, who is twelve, says this keeps out the dust. The cabin is small — no bigger than our carriage house back home. George seems proud that it has a "real door" and two glass windows, and that part of the floor is covered with a rug of braided rags.

The cabin is a square. It has a fireplace. An oven stands in a corner. They call this corner the kitchen. Shelves on the wall serve for a pantry. A quilt hangs from the rafters. Behind it is Aunt Margaret and Uncle Aubert's bed. George and Charlie and John sleep in the loft. And that is all there is of the cabin.

Aunt Margaret fixed us corn cakes and bacon for supper. I offered to set the table. Then I looked around. There was no table!

Aunt Margaret laughed. She picked up her wash-tub from where it hung on the wall. She set it upside down on the floor. That was our table. We sat around it on overturned buckets. We ate on tin plates. Aunt Margaret said that every bit of her china broke on the way to Kansas.

Uncle Aubert said that for now, I will sleep on a bed of "prairie feathers." He sent Charlie and John out to get a big load of hay. They piled half of it on the floor. Aunt Margaret laid two quilts on top. Then the boys piled the rest of the hay onto the quilts. I crawled between the two quilts. The hay smelled so sweet. It was as snug as a real feather bed.

Pres scrambled up the ladder to sleep in the loft with his cousins. Charlie is eight. John is six. Pres is seven, so he fits right between them.

I fell asleep listening to chirping crickets and to the low sounds of grown-ups talking. Uncle Aubert talked of owning land. Dr. Baer talked of voting to make Kansas a free state. Aunt Margaret said it was a great pity that women could not vote in elections.

This morning Pres and I hugged "our

dear Bear" good-bye. Then Ruby and Blanco took him off to Neosho and the vegetarians.

Later

I have written to Mother and Father. Uncle Aubert will take my letter to Lawrence. He says it will go out on the next wagon east. Uncle Aubert says he will see whether a letter has come from Father.

Pres told me he was going with Charlie and John to gather "buffalo chips." I wanted to ask what buffalo chips were, but Pres ran off too fast.

George showed me around outside. Uncle Albert has claimed 160 acres of land. To keep it, he had to build a cabin and he must farm the land. Behind the log cabin is a small barn. It is made of prairie-soil bricks, called "sod."

An ox named Kip and a black-and-white milk cow called Mollie live in the barn. Mollie is very fat. George says she will give birth to a calf this summer.

There is a stream nearby. And a grove of trees. George says this makes it a very good claim. He showed me his father's cornfield. The corn is up to my shoulder now.

George showed me Aunt Margaret's garden near the cabin. She is growing potatoes, carrots, watermelons, pumpkins, and squash.

The little boys came back from the prairie with six flour sacks of "buffalo chips" — also known as buffalo dung! George told me they dry it in the sacks all summer and then burn it for fuel all winter. I am very thankful that I will not be in Kansas for the winter.

Later

We have planted the baby apple trees beside the cabin. We spaced them apart with plenty of room to grow. I dug the holes. Aunt Margaret shook her head at me, digging in my lilac silk. She says she will soon make me a prairie dress. The boys ran down to the creek. They brought back buckets of water and watered the trees. I think Mother would be happy to see part of her garden growing in Kansas.

Later

Uncle Aubert came back from Lawrence. There was no letter from Father.

June 8, 1856

There is no church nearby, so we held our own worship this morning. We stood in a circle, holding hands. Uncle Aubert said the Twenty-third Psalm. Then we each prayed silently. I said my usual: *Dear Lord, please help Mother and Grace to get well!*

Pres told me he loves Kansas. He loves running outside all day. He loves flying his kite in the wind. He even loves gathering buffalo chips! He wishes we never had to go home again.

I said Kansas is the end of the earth.

June 10, 1856

I have a little room of my own! Uncle Aubert fastened an oak plank to the wall with wooden pegs. It is like a shelf, only wider.

Aunt Margaret and I stuffed a mattress ticking with hay. We tied this hay mattress on top of the wide shelf. Aunt Margaret gave me a ticking stuffed with chicken feathers, too. She says I can sleep on top of the feather bed in the warm weather — and crawl under it when it gets cold. I reminded her that I am staying only for the summer. I will not be here when the weather turns cold.

Uncle Aubert hung a quilt from the rafters. That is my "wall." We put my trunk beside my bed for a table. I put a candle and my diary on it. It is a cozy little room.

June 11, 1856

I awoke in the night to yellow eyes staring at me! I screamed. The eyes vanished. Aunt Margaret came running. "A wolf was here!" I cried. Aunt Margaret reached under my bed.

She picked up a gray cat. "Here is your wolf," she said. The cat's name is Mouser. I stroked her, and she purred like the engine of *The Kansas Hopeful.*

Pres, Charlie, and John followed me around all day today, howling like wolves. At last George made them stop their teasing. George is serious and a good help to his father. But Charlie and John are as wild as Pres.

June 12, 1856

Aunt Margaret hitched Kip to the oxcart this morning. She put the wash-tub in the cart, and all the dirty clothes. I went with her down to the stream. We walked through the prairie grass that goes on and on, as far as I can see.

Mouser came, too. She was hidden in the tall grass. We could see only the grass tops parting as she ran.

At the stream, we took off our shoes and stockings. Then Aunt Margaret took off her skirt. I gasped! She wore only her bodice and pantalettes! Aunt Margaret laughed. She said she favored the new style, started by Amelia Bloomer. Mrs. Bloomer believes that women should not have to wear heavy skirts and many petticoats. She believes women need clothes that make it easy for them to move when they work. So Mrs. Bloomer has invented "bloomers." They look like men's wide-legged trousers, gathered at the ankles.

Aunt Margaret working in her pantalettes! Mother would say she is a disgrace.

But Mother is not in Kansas.

I took off my skirt.

Aunt Margaret and I waded into the cold, clear water. We filled up the wash-tub. Aunt Margaret poured in a thick, strong-smelling soap that she had made herself. Then she put in the white clothing. She scrubbed and kneaded them in the suds. (No wonder her hands are red!) I helped her wring out the soapy water from the clothes. While she washed the dark clothing, I rinsed the white clothes in the stream. I waded up to my knees. How good it was to have a cool job on such a hot day!

When the clothes were rinsed, we wrung them out and spread them on the grass to dry.

While the clothes dried, Aunt Margaret and I lay on our backs and watched the clouds. They were white and fleecy, like lambs blowing across the sky. Far away we saw a dark cloud. In no time, the wind blew it over our heads. With a clap of thunder, that cloud let loose a flood of rain. Aunt Margaret and I ran around picking up the clothes from the grass. But we could not run fast enough. When the storm was over, all the clothes were streaked with mud. We had to start wash day all over again.

Mouser appeared after the storm. There was not a drop of water on her.

June 13, 1856

Aunt Margaret was stirring up corn cakes for lunch. She asked me to season the batter. I put in a pinch of salt. Then I reached for a shaker labeled PEPPER. Aunt Margaret quickly took the shaker from my hand. She unscrewed the lid. She showed me that this pepper is bright red. This is Aunt Margaret's just-in-case pepper. Just in case a Border Ruffian or an unfriendly Indian or a bear ever comes into the cabin, she will give him a face full of fiery red-hot pepper.

Later

Something terrible has happened! We saw what looked like a rain cloud coming. But it was a cloud of grasshoppers. They settled in Uncle Aubert's cornfield. In no time, they stripped the leaves off every plant. The whole crop is ruined.

Uncle Aubert has gone off on a walk by himself. George tried to run after him. But Aunt Margaret held him back. She said that Uncle Aubert needs time alone before he will be fit company.

June 15, 1856

I have a friend! Her name is Lily Vanbeek. She is eleven. But she is small for her age, so we are the same size. Lily has brown braids and freckled cheeks. I did not realize how lonely I have been for a friend.

Lily's family lives on the claim nearest this one. It is one mile away. Last night the Vanbeeks came for a "potluck" supper. Aunt Margaret says whatever we are lucky enough to have, we throw into the pot.

The Vanbeeks brought potatoes and pork for the pot and fried apples for dessert. They moved to Kansas from Minnesota. Lily has three older brothers and three younger brothers. She and I are both so happy to have another girl to talk to.

I wore my cream silk dress to dinner. Lily said she has never had a silk dress. She has only the blue-and-brown checked gingham dress she had on. And a green-and-brown checkered gingham for Sunday. I told her that I lacked prairie clothes. And Lily came up with the best plan!

We ran into my little room. We slipped out of our own dresses. We put on each other's clothes. Lily's gingham dress felt so soft and comfortable. We ran out. Uncle Aubert pretended he could not tell which of us was Lily and which was Meg.

Mr. Vanbeek took up his fiddle then. Aunt Margaret got out her tambourine. They played and the rest of us danced. We hooked elbows with partner after partner and swung around and around. (I think George liked having Lily for his partner.) Pres and John swung so wildly they felt sick to their stomachs and had to go outside. We danced until we collapsed onto the rug.

Then Mrs. Vanbeek began singing. She sang "Call to Kansas!" It made me miss our "old Bear."

At last Mrs. Vanbeek said they had best be getting home. Lily and I had to trade back our dresses. By the door, the grown-ups grew serious. They whispered about someone named Del. Mr. Vanbeek said the marshall had his eye on their cabin, and that he was looking for any sign of a runaway — Del would not be safe there much longer. Mrs. Vanbeek said something about the Underground Railroad and Canada.

Aunt Margaret is calling me to worship. I wonder who Del is?

Later

My prayer has not changed. After worship, I took out the pictures of Mother and Father and Grace and Nellie. I miss them all so much it makes my head ache.

Later

Uncle Aubert is worried about Mollie. She has lain down on the floor of the barn. She will not get up, even to graze. Charlie and John must take grass and water to her. I heard Aunt Margaret say that if they lost the cow, it would be a hard winter.

June 17, 1856

Aunt Margaret is making my prairie dress. She says she will show me how to stitch hems. It is made from tan cotton cloth with small blue flowers. It is not at all fashionable. But it is just right for Kansas.

June 18, 1856

Pres crawled into the shelf bed with me early this morning. He shook and said he was cold. But his head was burning hot.

Aunt Margaret put a wet cloth on his forehead. She told me not to worry — her own boys have come down with the shakes before. "And look at them now," she said.

June 19, 1856

I sit by my brother on my bed. I sponge his hot, red face and his skinny little arms. It is frightening to see him lie so still. Pres is never still.

How could I ever have wished that Pres would come down sick? I never meant it in my heart.

June 20, 1856

Pres has not eaten in three days. If only Dr. Baer were here. He would know what to do.

Pres sleeps in my shelf bed. So Charlie and John made me a prairie feather bed on the floor of my room. Aunt Margaret tells me to get some sleep, or I shall get sick, too. But how can I close my eyes? I must watch over Pres.

June 21, 1856

Uncle Aubert brought home a letter from Father. But it was the letter he wrote a month ago, before Pres and I left St. Louis. Uncle Aubert says the fighting around Lawrence makes the mail service unpredictable.

Later

Preston thrashes around so. The bed ticking is soaking wet. He says crazy things about riverboat gamblers. Aunt Margaret says it is the fever talking.

Later

Preston's fever has broken! This afternoon he sat up in bed. He hollered, "Four feet, five feet, no bottom!" And he sank back down. I feared that the fever had made him lose his mind. Then I felt his head. It was cool! Aunt Margaret says Pres will soon start to feel better.

June 22, 1856

Preston is pale and thin. But he is kicking off the covers. He badly wants to get out of bed. Aunt Margaret says I mustn't let him. I am so thankful he is better.

More good news! Mollie has given birth to twins! Both calves are healthy and drinking Mollie's milk.

We worshiped longer than usual today. We have much to be thankful for.

June 25, 1856

Late last night there was a knock on the door. It was Theo Vanbeek, Lily's oldest brother. Theo said now the marshall has a posse with him. The men ride by their cabin. They speak loudly, so the Vanbeeks can hear them. They talk about a man who wants his "property" back.

Theo said he made sure he was not seen coming to our cabin. He asked if Del might stay with us until the Underground Railroad comes for her.

Aunt Margaret and Uncle Aubert both said yes.

Theo asked if they knew the punishment for hiding a runaway slave.

Uncle Aubert nodded. If caught, he would have to pay one thousand dollars and spend six months in prison.

One thousand dollars! Uncle Aubert does not have that much money. And what if he went to prison? What would become of his family?

But Aunt Margaret said, "It is the right thing to do."

Uncle Aubert said, "The only thing."

Theo said his family would come over tonight for supper. And that Del would be with them. Then he slipped out of our cabin and disappeared into the night.

My heart beats like a drum. A runaway slave, coming here. To this tiny cabin! Wherever can we hide her?

Later

No one says much now. Everyone walks around the cabin. We all hope to discover some small hiding space we never noticed before.

Pres is so pale. His poor arms are as skinny as twigs. But he is wild again. Aunt Margaret says he may *not* get out of bed. So he stands on his head in bed. He puts his feet against the wall. He stays there until his face turns purple. We all scold him. But he cannot hold still.

We have a bigger worry. Del is coming tonight, and there is still no place to hide her.

Later

Pres has given us an idea. I came into my room with soup for him. But he was not in bed. When I called his name, there was no answer. Suddenly Pres sprang up from under the feather bed, shouting, "No bottom!" I was so startled! I nearly spilled the soup. Then I thought, *If Pres can disappear under the feather bed . . .*

Later

The Vanbeeks came for supper in the pouring rain. There are so many of them, they knew the marshall would not notice one extra passenger in the wagon. They were all bundled up against the rain. The whole family came into our cabin together in a bunch. Then they stepped apart. And there was Del. She wore a man's hat. A scarf was wound around her throat and covered half of her face. She had on a long-sleeved man's shirt, gloves, trousers, and boots. She took off her hat and unwound her scarf. I saw that she was not very big. And that she had a deep scar on her forehead.

Quickly, Aunt Margaret took Del into my little room. She explained the plan. How, if the marshall came, Del could hide between the straw mattress and the feather bed. How Pres would play sick. How he would lie on top of the feather bed, covered in quilts.

Del nodded. She smiled at Pres. She said she hoped he would not mind a lump in his bed. Pres bounced on the bed. He said he liked lumps.

I scolded Pres for bouncing. I said that this was not a game. This was the most important thing he would ever do. That if the marshall came, he must pretend to be asleep and not move a muscle. Pres said he understood. But he bounced as he said it.

Then Del sat down on my trunk. She said if the marshall came, she knew Pres would do just fine.

Pres nodded. But he kept on bouncing.

We had our potluck supper. Del said she wanted to stay in my room and keep Pres company. So Lily and I took a plate to her. Then the rest of us ate and sang and danced. If the marshall and his posse looked in through the windows, they would have seen only two families, having fun.

One by one, the Vanbeeks slipped into my room to say good-bye to Del. Lily cried when she hugged her. Then the Vanbeeks left our cabin, all in a bunch again.

Now the house is quiet. The dishes are done. I have split my prairie feather bed in two. I am sleeping on one half. Del is next to me on the other. Uncle Aubert says he and George will take turns keeping watch through the night.

I am about to blow out my candle.

What will this night bring?

June 26, 1856

Nothing happened in the night.

This morning, Aunt Margaret and I loaded the tub and the wash onto Kip's oxcart as usual. We went down to the stream as usual. We washed the clothes as usual. We are all doing everything as usual. If any riders come by, they will not guess that anything is unusual at all.

Here is the hardest part: Pres must stay inside. He is supposed to be sick. If the marshall rides by, he must not see Pres outside playing. Staying inside is hard for Pres. And I am very worried that if the marshall comes, Pres will not be able to hold still.

Del is so gentle. I cannot stand to think that she might be sold, with her legs in chains. I hate to think how she got the awful scar on her forehead. And I am proud of Uncle Aubert and Aunt Margaret for taking her in. I am proud that we are a "station" on the Underground Railroad.

June 27, 1856

The marshall and his men came last night!

George had been watching at the window. There was no moon. So he did not see the riders until they had almost reached the cabin.

George rushed to my room. He whispered, "Marshall!"

Del sprang up. I lifted Pres. Del dove under

his feather bed. I put Pres down again and straightened his covers.

Quickly, I shoved the straw from Del's bed back in with the straw from mine. I lay down and drew up the quilts.

Then came a pounding on the door.

Uncle Aubert lit a candle. George opened the door. I heard the marshall's voice. He said that he had reason to believe we were holding another man's property. He said that he and his men had come to search the cabin.

Uncle Aubert said, "Search if you must. We have nothing here that belongs to any other man."

I have never been so frightened. The men's boots pounded loudly on the wooden floors.

I lay shivering. I heard Uncle Aubert tell the marshall that his nephew was very ill.

Suddenly my quilt wall was swept aside. Above me stood the marshall. His lantern shone in my eyes. I got to my feet. I squinted into the light.

I said, "Uncle?"

Uncle Aubert said the marshall wanted to look around.

The marshall held his lantern over Pres.

Pres's eyelids fluttered.

I prayed, *Please, Lord, do not let Pres give Del away!*

I looked up into the marshall's face. It was the face of a hunter. He was hunting Del. To take her back to slavery! I felt anger boil up inside me.

The marshall asked, "What ails the boy?"

My anger made me brave. I spoke. I said that my brother had a fever. That he could keep nothing in his stomach. That I feared that he had caught the terrible sickness that had killed so many folks on our riverboat.

The marshall quickly stepped back from

the bed. He lowered his lantern. Then he turned and went back out to the main part of the cabin.

The searchers kicked at the sacks of buffalo chips by the fireplace. They looked behind the oven. One of them poked the barrel of his rifle up the chimney. But they found nothing.

The marshall told Uncle Aubert that they would be watching us. Then he and his men left.

For a minute, no one moved. Then Del lifted a corner of the feather bed to get some air. I took my brother's hand. I squeezed it. Pres had held as still as a statue.

Later

More knocking sounded on the door!
My heart began to pound.

Uncle Aubert opened the door. I heard him say, "Thank heaven!"

It was the "conductors" from the Underground Railroad.

Everything was a rush then. These men had been waiting down by the creek. Their scout saw the marshall and his men come into our cabin. He saw them come out and ride off again. He followed them. Not far away, the marshall and his men had split up to go home. The scout said they would not come back tonight.

Del took my hand. And Pres's. She said she would never forget our kindness. Then she wrapped the scarf around her head. She put on her coat and hat. And she was gone.

We watched from the window as her rescuers rushed her to a waiting hay wagon. A man with a pitchfork lifted up the hay. Del disappeared deep into it. The wagon pulled away. Now I was thankful for the moonless night.

June 28, 1856

It is a perfect Kansas morning. The sky is blue. The wind is soft. And Del is on her way to Canada!

Aunt Margaret said that Pres could go outside. With a whoop he ran out the door after George, Charlie, and John.

Uncle Aubert hitched Kip to the wagon. He drove to the Vanbeeks to let them know that all was well.

Aunt Margaret said she wanted to run down to the creek to gather watercress for supper. She asked me to start the johnnycake batter.

I was stirring the batter, humming to

myself. I never heard boots come up the steps. The first I knew that I had company was when a man's voice called, "Anybody home?"

I was alone in the cabin.

It was too late to hide.

Aunt Margaret had not bothered to bolt the door. It creaked open.

I gasped when I saw who stood in the doorway. The yellow-haired gambler from *The Kansas Hopeful*!

He stared at me.

I did the only thing I could think of.

I grabbed the just-in-case red-hot pepper.

I said, "Go away!"

The gambler grinned. Just the way he had grinned at Miss Annie Boone! He said he was looking for Aubert Parker.

How did he know my uncle's name? Had the marshall sent him? My head was spinning.

I held my pepper ready.

Then I heard Aunt Margaret call out, "Jasper!"

The gambler turned. The next thing I knew, Aunt Margaret had thrown her arms around him as if he were a long-lost friend.

Which is what he turned out to be.

Aunt Margaret told the gambler to come inside. She came in, too. When she saw me standing with the hot pepper shaker in my hand, she laughed so hard she had to sit down. She told the gambler he had just had a very narrow escape.

The yellow-haired gambler's name is Mr. Jasper Young. He was on the steamboat that brought Uncle Aubert and Aunt Margaret to Kansas. They became good friends. He will be staying with us in the cabin for a while.

Mr. Young is not a professional gambler. He only likes to play cards. He does not carry rifles or pistols inside his cases. He carries a camera. And lots of heavy camera equipment. Mr. Young is a wandering photographer. He says we are living an important part of history and he wants to capture it in photographs.

I wanted to believe him. But one thing bothered me.

"Why was Miss Annie Boone so angry at you?" I asked him. "Why did she run when she saw you?"

Mr. Young laughed. He said that he had taken her photograph. When she saw it, she yelled that it was a photograph of some wrinkled, toothless old lady. But it sure wasn't a photograph of Miss Annie Boone. And she chased him out of her cabin.

Mr. Young has offered to take my photograph.

July 1, 1856

We have been so busy! I have not had a moment to write. Aunt Margaret and I have been making pies. It seems we will need many when we go to the big Fourth of July pic-nic just outside of Lawrence. I fear my fingers may stay blue forever from picking so many blueberries.

July 2, 1856

The best thing in the world has happened! Better than twin calves. Better than a new friend. Better even than a letter from Father!

Aunt Margaret and I were in the kitchen this afternoon. We were baking pies. It was a hot, hot day. Our cabin was steaming. When the pies were ready to bake, Aunt Margaret lit the oven. The burning wood made the cabin even hotter. We could barely stand the heat.

Uncle Aubert had gone to Lawrence. The boys were out collecting wood. So Aunt Margaret and I took off our skirts. We worked in our camisoles and pantalettes. Our wet hair stuck to our faces. Flour from the piecrusts stuck to us all over. We wanted to be finished, so we worked fast.

Then, BANG! Aunt Margaret dropped a whole pie on the floor.

I saw that she was not looking at the pie. She was staring at the door.

My first thought was Border Ruffians! Or a bear! Then I looked. And if I had been holding a pie, I would have dropped it, too.

In the doorway stood Mother and Grace! At first I thought I was seeing things — that the heat had made me lose my senses.

Then Mother stepped into the cabin. She held my sister's hand. "Well, Grace," she said. "We surely have come to the end of the earth."

Oh, how we hugged and kissed. I cried. So did Aunt Margaret. I held Grace in my lap for the longest time. My prayers have been answered!

Aunt Margaret and I rinsed off with water from the bucket. We put on our skirts. Then we went outside, where we might catch a breeze, to listen to Mother's story. When Mother saw her baby apple trees planted beside the cabin, she broke down and cried, too.

Mother told us that Grace had recovered quickly. But she herself was ill for a long time. She said that she decided something while lying in her sick bed. She would never again spend a summer in St. Louis worrying that her children might die of cholera.

As soon as Mother recovered, she and Grace traveled up the Missouri River on *The*

Silver Cloud. In Kansas City, they hired a carriage for the trip to our cabin.

Father is still in St. Louis. He will sell his business and the house. He is having the furniture packed and shipped to Kansas.

Mother asked Nellie to come to Kansas, too. But she said she has saved a good amount of money working for us. And it seems a certain Sean O'Brien from Ireland is waiting for her in New York City. So Mother put her on a train bound for New York.

The boys came home for dinner. When Pres saw Mother, he let out such a whoop. Mother held him in her lap while she told him that our family hopes to buy a claim near Aunt Margaret and Uncle Aubert. We are going to live in Kansas.

Preston shouted out, "Amen!"

July 3, 1856

Mother, Grace, and I went down to the stream this morning. Mouser came, too. We took a pic-nic.

I waded in the cool water with Grace while Mother read my diary. When she read about Grigg's Hotel, she said, "Oh, my!" She read all the way to the end, then said I had done a fine job of writing my adventures. It made me so happy to hear it!

July 4, 1856

We have come to the Lawrence Pic-nic. Everyone has brought all sorts of food. We will all share our food with everyone else at the pic-nic. I do believe half of Kansas Territory is here. There are folks dressed in silks, like

Mother. There are folks dressed in cotton, like me. (Aunt Margaret finished my prairie dress last night!) Some folks are wearing buckskin and others, flour-sack trousers. There are Delawares wrapped in bright red blankets and men in denim trousers and leather hats. Everyone seems to want to get along on the Fourth of July.

We are lucky to have found a shady spot to spread our quilts. The Vanbeeks have their quilts spread next to ours.

Mother, Aunt Margaret, and I put our pies on the long table. I think there is enough food on it to feed the whole territory!

I have been sitting on our quilt, writing, but Pres is pulling me to my feet. He says it is time to eat. He says we must hurry! I say that, with our riverboat manners, we need not worry about missing dinner.

Later

What a feast! There was barbecued buffalo and deer, barbecued lamb and fresh ham. Even Dr. Baer and the Peach ladies could have had a vegetarian feast on the corn cakes, mashed squash, diced potatoes, and salads of every sort. There were pies and cakes topped with ice cream, too. It tasted even better than the ice cream at Barnum's City Hotel.

This diary was to last me a year. But I have only one page left. I looked back at the first pages. I had to laugh at my idea of adventure! I need a new book now to write more Kansas adventures. For I will be here when the cold weather comes. I will warm myself by a buffalo-chip fire. I will sleep under a feather bed. I will go to school with Lily in Lawrence this fall.

Mr. Young, formerly known as the yellow-haired gambler, is calling us. He has set up his camera. He wants to take a picture of Uncle Aubert, Aunt Margaret, George, Charlie, John, Mother, Pres, Grace, all the many Vanbeeks, and me. Next year, Father will be here to be in the picture, too.

The speeches are starting now. The crowd is quieting. A man has stepped onto a platform. He is reading from the Declaration of Independence. These lines from it seem a fine way to end my diary: *We hold these truths to be self-evident, that all men are created equal, that they are endowed by their Creator with certain unalienable Rights, that among these are Life, Liberty, and the pursuit of Happiness.*

Amen!

Life in America
in 1856

Historical Note

In 1856, Missouri was a state in the United States. St. Louis was its largest city, with 122,000 people. St. Louis factories made engines, railroad cars, soap, candles, and chemicals. Black smoke billowed out of factory smokestacks into the sky. The air was full of soot and dirt.

A view of St. Louis, Missouri, in the 1850s.

Yet St. Louis was not all soot and smoke. It also had fine hotels. Opera singers came from Europe to sing in its beautiful theaters. Wealthy families lived in grand houses. They wore fancy clothes made of silk and linen.

Servants helped care for the grand houses and the people who lived in them. They often lived in small rooms on the top floor of the house. Although most servants were paid for their work, nearly 2,000 people in St. Louis in 1856 were slaves who worked for no pay. There were people who thought of slaves as property. Several times a year, slaves stood on the steps of the Courthouse to be sold.

A *slave auction*.

Slavery was not against the law in Missouri in 1856 but many believed it was a terrible evil. These "abolitionists" worked to pass laws against slavery. And many of them helped slaves escape to Canada on the Underground Railroad.

More than 4,000 people in St. Louis died in the great cholera epidemic of 1849. Cholera is caused by dirty drinking water and contaminated food. But back then, no one knew the cause. Every summer for years, cholera broke out in St. Louis.

The St. Louis riverfront was lined with many huge steamboats known as "floating palaces." Some had grand staircases and carpeted lounges.

The "floating palace" steamboats docked at St. Louis.

The boats were powered by hot wood fires that boiled water under great pressure to make steam. Sometimes the boilers exploded and the boats caught fire. Riverboat travel was both exciting and dangerous.

In 1856, it took about six days to travel on a floating palace from St. Louis to Kansas City. West of Kansas City lay Kansas Territory. People went there for the chance to own land. Others went for the adventure. Still others went because of slavery.

A sod house in Kansas.

At this time, about half the states in the United States allowed slavery. The other half did not. By 1856, everyone knew that Kansas would soon become a state. But would it be a free state? Or would it allow slavery? Congress said that people in Kansas should vote to decide.

Some men from the South came to Kansas only temporarily. They were called Border Ruffians. They came by the thousands over the border into Kansas. They roved in gangs, and were dangerous outlaws. They went to vote, saying that they lived in Kansas. They voted for Kansas to allow slavery. And then they went back home again. They figured that the more slave states there were, the harder it would be to end slavery. In the years right before the Civil War, Kansas Territory turned into

Border Ruffians.

a terrible battleground. The Free Staters, northerners who went to Kansas, fought the Border Ruffians. Many died in the fighting.

Life in Kansas Territory held other dangers as well. There were fierce thunderstorms. Plagues of grasshoppers ate the crops. The summers were burning hot and dry. Winters brought blizzards and freezing cold. Yet even though the Kansas prairie of 1856 was a hard place to live, many loved living in its endless seas of grass, and breathing its fresh, clean air. They would not have traded their lives on the prairie for anything.

Burning fields to kill grasshoppers.

About the Author

Kate McMullan says, "I grew up in St. Louis, Missouri, and was a great Mark Twain fan. His stories always made me wish I could travel back in time and take a ride on a steamboat. I loved writing about Meg's journey because it gave me a feel for what an 1856 ride up the wild Missouri River must have been like."

Kate McMullan has written more than fifty books for children, including the best-selling *If You Were My Bunny* and *The Story of Harriet Tubman, Conductor on the Underground Railroad*. She teaches writing for children in the Master of Fine Arts program at the New

School University, and lives with her daughter and her husband, the noted illustrator James McMullan, in New York City and Sag Harbor, Long Island.

Acknowledgments

The author would like to thank her editors, Beth Levine and Amy Griffin, for their wise guidance with this project. She would also like to thank Jenny Vaughn, Marky Shapleigh, Susan Craig, and Jane Courter; The Campbell House Museum in St. Louis, Missouri; and Deborah M. White of the Lawrence Visitor Center. She is especially grateful to Judith M. Sweets of the Watkins Community Museum of History in Lawrence, Kansas, for her critical reading of the manuscript. She would like to acknowledge her debt to two diarists who traveled to Kansas in the 1850s: Mrs. Miriam Davis Colt and the Reverend Richard Cordley.

Grateful acknowledgment is made for permission to reprint the following:

page 97: View of St. Louis, State Historical Society of Missouri, Columbia.

page 98: Slave auction, State Historical Society of Missouri, Columbia.

page 99: Floating palace, North Wind Picture Archives.

page 100: Sod house, North Wind Picture Archives.

page 101: Border Ruffians, State Historical Society of Missouri, Columbia.

page 102: Burning the fields, The Kansas State Historical Society, Topeka, Kansas.

Other books in the My America series

Our Strange New Land
Elizabeth's Diary
by Patricia Hermes

The Starving Time
Elizabeth's Diary, Book Two
by Patricia Hermes

My Brother's Keeper
Virginia's Diary
by Mary Pope Osborne

After the Rain
Virginia's Diary, Book Two
by Mary Pope Osborne

Five Smooth Stones
Hope's Diary
by Kristiana Gregory

Westward to Home
Joshua's Diary
by Patricia Hermes

Freedom's Wings
Corey's Diary
by Sharon Dennis Wyeth

For Cathee Adderton Zebell,
with great affection and gratitude

While the events described and some of the characters in this book
may be based on actual historical events and real people, Margaret
Cora Wells is a fictional character, created by the author, and her
diary is a work of fiction.

Library of Congress Cataloging-in-Publication Data
McMullan, Kate.
As far as I can see : Meg's diary / by Kate McMullan.
p.   cm. — (My America)
Summary: In her diary for 1856, nine-year-old Meg describes the long, dangerous journey she
and her younger brother make from Missouri to Kansas, as well as the new life they find there.
ISBN 0-439-18895-4
[1. Frontier and pioneer life — Fiction. 2. Diaries — Fiction.]   I. Title.   II. Series.
PZ7.M47879 As 2001
[Fic] — dc21   00-067026
CIP AC

10 9 8 7 6 5 4 3 2 1   01 02 03 04 05

The display type was set in Rogers.
The text type was set in Goudy.
Photo research by Zoe Moffitt
Book design by Elizabeth B. Parisi

Printed in the U.S.A. 23
First edition, September 2001